for Santa and his helpers

Atheneum Books for Young Readers
An imprint of Simon & Schuster Children's Publishing Division
1230 Avenue of the Americas, New York, New York 10020

Text copyright © 2002 by Petra Mathers
Illustrations copyright © 2002 by Petra Mathers

Book design by Ann Bobco

The text for this book is set in Deepdene.
The illustrations for this book are rendered in watercolor.

Printed in Hong Kong
First Edition
2 4 6 8 10 9 7 5 3 1

Library of Congress Cataloging-in-Publication Data
Mathers, Petra
Herbie's secret Santa / Petra Mathers.—1st ed.
p. cm.
"An Anne Schwartz book."
Summary: As Lottie and Herbie get ready for Christmas, Herbie does something he regrets and cannot enjoy the holiday until he tells Lottie about it.
ISBN 0-689-83550-7
[1. Birds—Fiction. 2. Honesty—Fiction. 3. Christmas—Fiction. 4. Friendship—Fiction.] I. Title.
PZ7.M42475 He 2002
[E]—dc21
2001055274

Herbie's Secret Santa

by petra mathers

An Anne Schwartz Book
ATHENEUM BOOKS FOR YOUNG READERS
New York London Toronto Sydney Singapore

It was three days before Christmas.
Lottie was waiting for her best friend, Herbie, to help her buy the tree.
I hope the sky clears so we can see the Christmas Star, she thought.

"I'm a happy Santa, and hum a happy hum,
I'm on my way to Lottie's,
teedle-merry-dum."

"Hi, Lottie, did you wrap my present
yet?" Herbie asked.
"What present?" said Lottie.

"I wrapped yours," said Herbie.
"It's in my pocket. Want to know what
   letter it starts with?"
"No, thank you," said Lottie.

"It starts with *s*," said Herbie.
"Hmm," said Lottie, "is it sassafras?
   I love sassafras."
"Oh, Lottie," said Herbie.

It was a busy day in Oysterville. Vince and Dodo, friends from
Crook Road, were in line at the post office.
"Yoo-hoo, see you Christmas!" Dodo cried. "Vince is making
Christmas pickles. Come early!"

Things were quiet at the tree lot.
"Oh Lottie, look, the Christmas trees are sleeping," said Herbie.
"Go ahead and wake one up, Mr. Kringle," said the tree man.

The door to the bakery was open.
Inside it smelled delicious.
"Hey, wait for me," said Herbie.

"Looky who's here," Baba said.
"Lottie and Santa."
"Christmas is near. You must be busy,
   Santa," said Ali. Herbie did not hear her.

Just look at these cookies—
little Santas, just like me, Herbie thought.

Mmmh, that frosting, all red and shiny. Maybe I could pick one up and give it just a tiny lick.

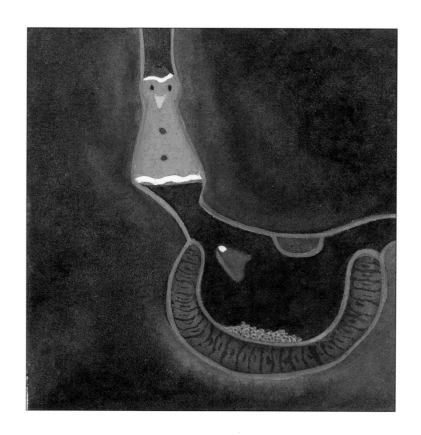

One lick and then another.
OH NO. The cookie broke. What now?
"Time to go, dear," Lottie called.

Herbie panicked.
He swallowed the cookie whole.
It hurt all the way down to his stomach.

"Happy, happy," Ali and Baba said.
"Merry, merry," said Lottie.
  Herbie couldn't get a word out.

At Mabel's Greens he stayed outside.
"Don't you look sweet, li'l Santa,"
someone said.
She's talking to the cookie, Herbie thought.

On the way home Herbie felt like everyone was staring at him,
and he knew why:
They had X-ray vision and could see the cookie.

When they finally reached Lottie's,
Herbie was hot and prickly.
"Just get inside, you dumb tree," he mumbled.

"Let's sing 'Jingle Bells,'" said Lottie.
"I want to go home," said Herbie.

"Don't catch cold. See you tomorrow, Santa," Lottie called after him.

"I'm no Santa," said Herbie and buried his hat and boots.

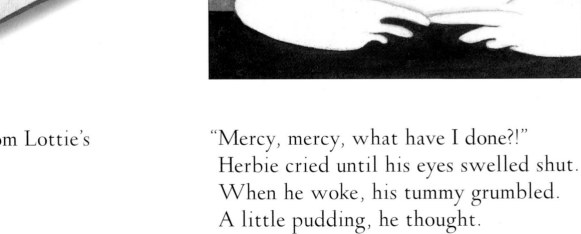

At home he found a card from Lottie's Aunt Mattie.

"Mercy, mercy, what have I done?!" Herbie cried until his eyes swelled shut. When he woke, his tummy grumbled. A little pudding, he thought.

His tummy growled.
"Be quiet," said Herbie. "You're only
a cookie, not even a very big one, and
there were lots left just like you."

But he couldn't get comfy.
"Thief, thief," a little voice whispered.
"Am not," said Herbie. "I'll pay for you
tomorrow."

Early the next morning Herbie waited outside the bakery.
I could say the cookie fell into my pocket, he thought.
When Baba came out, Herbie ducked.
"Ali, look, isn't that Herbie over there? But where is his outfit?"

"Hey Herbie, what happened to Santa?"
"They know," Herbie gasped and ran . . .

. . . all the way to Lottie's house.
"Help!" he cried.

"Oh, Herbie," said Lottie when he finished
his story, "you and your bottomless belly."
"I know, I'm so ashamed. I'll go right now
and tell everything," said Herbie.

Herbie ran so fast his belly shook.
He could feel the cookie jumping
up and down.

"Ihh-a stolehha-ha a Santahh, Imha sorryhh."
There was an awful silence.

"I'll never do it again. I can't eat, I can't sleep,
  and now you don't like me anymore," wailed Herbie.
"I'm glad you told us," said Ali. "That was brave."
"So do you think some day you will like me again?" Herbie asked.

"After Christmas," Baba said at last.
"After Christmas, when you come in, I'll say,
'Herbie, how nice to see you, have a cookie.'"

Herbie felt relieved.
But then he thought of Lottie.
Am I still her best friend? he wondered.

"There you are," a voice said. "Better?"
"Oh Lottie, yes, much better."

"Let's find the Christmas Star," said Herbie.
"In that sky?" said Lottie. "I don't think we can.

She sounds sad, thought Herbie.
And then in his pocket
he felt what had been there all along.
His present for Lottie.

"Oh yes we can!" he shouted.
"Right here, this is our Christmas Star,
the one I made for you."

"Merry Christmas, Lottie, Merry Christmas, World,
you most wonderful World in the World!"

THE END